World of Insects

Cockroaches

by Deirdre A. Prischmann

Consultant:
Gary A. Dunn, MS, Director of Education
Young Entomologists' Society, Inc.
Minibeast Zooseum and Education Center
Lansing, Michigan

Mankato, Minnesota

Bridgestone Books are published by Capstone Press,
151 Good Counsel Drive, P.O. Box 669, Mankato, Minnesota 56002.
www.capstonepress.com

Copyright © 2006 by Capstone Press. All rights reserved.
No part of this publication may be reproduced in whole or in part, or stored in a retrieval system, or transmitted in any form or by any means, electronic, mechanical, photocopying, recording, or otherwise, without written permission of the publisher.
For information regarding permission, write to Capstone Press,
151 Good Counsel Drive, P.O. Box 669, Dept. R, Mankato, Minnesota 56002.
Printed in the United States of America

Library of Congress Cataloging-in-Publication Data
Prischmann, Deirdre A.
    Cockroaches / by Deirdre A. Prischmann.
       p. cm.—(Bridgestone Books. World of insects)
       Summary: "A brief introduction to cockroaches, discussing their characteristics, habitat, life cycle, and predators. Includes a range map, life cycle illustration, and amazing facts"—Provided by publisher.
       Includes bibliographical references and index.
       ISBN 0-7368-4336-1 (hardcover)
       1. Cockroaches—Juvenile literature. I. Title. II. Series.
QL505.5.P75 2006
595.7'28—dc22   2004028518

Editorial Credits
Shari Joffe, editor; Jennifer Bergstrom, set designer; Biner Design, book designer;
    Patricia Rasch, illustrator; Jo Miller, photo researcher; Scott Thoms, photo editor

Photo Credits
Bruce Coleman Inc./C.B. Frith, 16; Kim Taylor, 12; Peter Ward, 10
Corbis/David Aubrey, 1
Dwight R. Kuhn, 4
Photo Researchers Inc., 6; Biophoto Associates, cover; J.H. Robinson, 18
UNICORN Stock Photos/Russell R. Grundke, 20

1 2 3 4 5 6   10 09 08 07 06 05

Table of Contents

Cockroaches 5

What Cockroaches Look Like 7

Cockroaches in the World 9

Cockroach Habitats 11

What Cockroaches Eat 13

Eggs and Nymphs 15

Molting into an Adult 17

Dangers to Cockroaches 19

Amazing Facts about Cockroaches 21

Glossary 22

Read More 23

Internet Sites 23

Index 24

Cockroaches

Cockroaches run fast, smell bad, and creep around at night. People often try to rid their homes of them. But cockroaches are survivors. They have been around much longer than people.

Cockroaches are insects related to termites and mantids. Like all insects, cockroaches have six legs, three body parts, and an **exoskeleton**. The exoskeleton protects the insect's body.

◀ Cockroaches, like this one crawling on some celery, are known for being pests.

What Cockroaches Look Like

Cockroaches have flat, oval bodies made up of three parts. The head is one part. On its head, a cockroach has eyes, long **antennae**, and mouthparts. Its legs and four wings attach to the middle part, or **thorax**. The end part, or **abdomen**, holds the stomach and heart-like pump.

A cockroach may be as short as a pencil eraser or as long as ten pencil erasers. Most cockroaches are brown or black, but some are green, red, or orange.

◄ Many kinds of cockroaches have wings but do not fly.

Cockroach Range Map

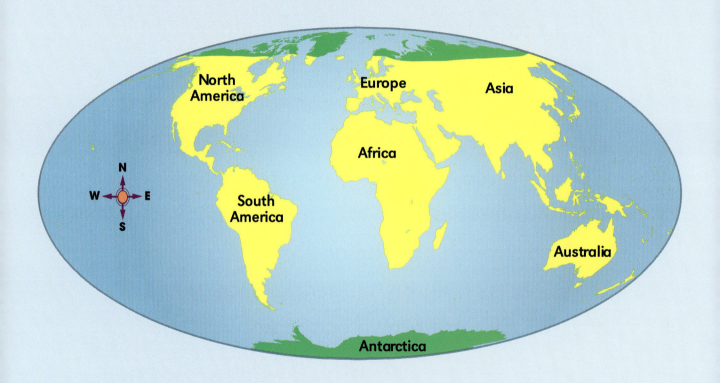

Where Cockroaches Live

Cockroaches in the World

More than 3,500 kinds of cockroaches live on earth. Cockroaches can be found all over the world. Most live in warm, moist areas. In the United States, many cockroaches live in Texas and Florida.

Cockroaches can survive in extreme places. Some live on cold mountaintops. Others live underground in caves. Some are found in hot, dry deserts. The only outdoor places too extreme for cockroaches are polar areas.

Cockroach Habitats

Most cockroaches live outdoors. Some live under leaves, tree bark, logs, or stones. Others dig into sand, dirt, or rotting wood. Some cockroaches even live in ant nests.

Only a few kinds of cockroaches live inside places built by people. German, American, and Oriental cockroaches climb walls and squeeze into cracks in houses. Cockroaches also live in sewers, restaurants, and stores.

◀ People think of cockroaches as indoor pests, but most types of cockroaches live outside.

What Cockroaches Eat

Many cockroaches eat dead and rotting plants. Brown-hooded cockroaches eat wood. Some cockroaches feed on fruit.

Cockroaches also eat dead insects and fish, animal hair, and animal waste. Sometimes cockroaches even eat their own eggs.

Cockroaches that live among people often feed on things made by humans. They eat paper, paste, paint, and plaster. They also eat people's food and clothes.

◀ Cockroaches that live in people's homes eat any kind of human food they can find.

The Life Cycle of a Cockroach

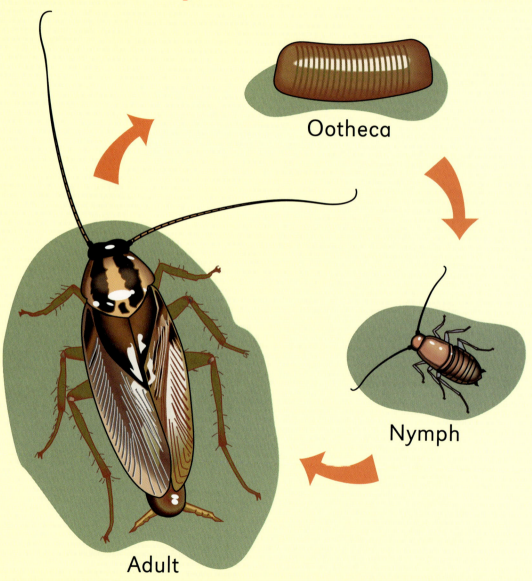

Eggs and Nymphs

Male and female cockroaches mate to produce young. After mating, the female cockroach lays an egg case, or **ootheca**. The ootheca holds 6 to 48 eggs. It is brown, leathery, and shaped like a bean.

When cockroach **nymphs** are ready to hatch, they push open the ootheca. The nymphs are soft and white at first. Later, they become darker. They look like small adults without wings. Cockroach nymphs can take care of themselves as soon as they hatch.

Molting into an Adult

As nymphs grow, they **molt**, or shed their exoskeleton, four or five times. Nymphs are white right after they molt. Their exoskeletons soon darken.

After their last molt, nymphs become adults. Some cockroaches change from eggs to adults in about two months. Others take nearly three years to become adults.

Cockroaches can live up to four years. Some females lay more than 1,000 eggs in their lifetimes.

◂ A newly molted white nymph stands next to its old exoskeleton.

Dangers to Cockroaches

Cockroaches face many dangers. Spiders, lizards, birds, and many other animals eat them. Many people poison or trap cockroaches to get rid of them.

Cockroaches have several defenses. They can run fast. Some hide from enemies by blending into their habitat. Others pretend to be dead.

Cockroaches have been on earth for more than 340 million years. Although many people dislike them, cockroaches are here to stay.

◀ A spider catches a cockroach in its web.

Amazing Facts about Cockroaches

- Some cockroaches make noises to scare enemies or get mates. Madagascar hissing cockroaches make noise by pushing air out of the breathing holes on their abdomens.
- Some cockroaches can live for a week without their heads.
- Cockroaches are among the fastest insects. Some cockroaches can run more than 50 inches (127 centimeters) per second.
- A young cockroach can squeeze into a crack as thin as a dime.

◄ The Madagascar hissing cockroach is a large, wingless cockroach that hisses when threatened.

Glossary

abdomen (AB-duh-muhn)—the end section of an insect's body

antenna (an-TEN-uh)—a feeler on an insect's head

exoskeleton (eks-oh-SKEL-uh-tuhn)—the hard outer covering of an insect

molt (MOHLT)—to shed an outer layer of skin, or exoskeleton, so a new exoskeleton can be seen

nymph (NIMF)—a young form of an insect; nymphs change into adults by molting several times.

ootheca (oh-uh-THEE-kuh)—an egg case made by a cockroach or mantid

thorax (THOR-aks)—the middle section of an insect's body; wings and legs are attached to the thorax.

Read More

Jacobs, Liza. *Cockroaches.* Wild Wild World. San Diego: Blackbirch Press, 2003.

Merrick, Patrick. *Cockroaches.* Naturebooks. Chanhassen, Minn.: Child's World, 2003.

Internet Sites

FactHound offers a safe, fun way to find Internet sites related to this book. All of the sites on FactHound have been researched by our staff.

Here's how:
1. Visit *www.facthound.com*
2. Type in this special code **0736843361** for age-appropriate sites. Or enter a search word related to this book for a more general search.
3. Click on the **Fetch It** button.

FactHound will fetch the best sites for you!

Index

abdomen, 7, 21
antennae, 7

body parts, 5, 7

dangers, 19
defenses, 19

eating, 13
eggs, 13, 15, 17
exoskeleton, 5, 17
eyes, 7

food, 13

habitats, 9, 11
head, 7, 21
hiding, 19
hissing, 21

legs, 5, 7
life cycle, 15, 17

mating, 15, 21
molting, 17
mouthparts, 7

night, 5
noises, 21
nymphs, 15, 17

ootheca, 15

people, 5, 11, 13, 19
plants, 13

range, 9
running, 19, 21

size, 7
stomach, 7

thorax, 7

wings, 7, 15